Three Little Hunters

by
W.G. Van de Hulst

illustrated by
Willem G. Van de Hulst, Jr.

INHERITANCE PUBLICATIONS
NEERLANDIA, ALBERTA, CANADA
PELLA, IOWA, U.S.A.

Library and Archives Canada Cataloguing in Publication
Hulst, W. G. van de (Willem Gerrit), 1879-1963
[Wilde jaggers. English]
    Three little hunters / by W.G. Van de Hulst ; illustrated by
Willem G. Van de Hulst, Jr. ; [translated by Harry der Nederlanden].
(Stories children love ; 11)
Translation of: De wilde jaggers.
Originally published: St. Catharines, Ontario : Paideia Press, 1979.
ISBN 978-1-928136-11-8 (pbk.)
        I. Hulst, Willem G. van de (Willem Gerrit), 1917-, illustrator
II. Nederlanden, Harry der, translator III. Title. IV. Title: Wilde
jaggers. English V. Series: Hulst, W. G. van de (Willem Gerrit), 1879-1963
Stories children love ; 11
PZ7.H873985Thr 2014   j839.313'62   C2014-903604-3

Library of Congress Cataloging-in-Publication Data
(applied for)

Originally published in Dutch as *De wilde jagers*
Cover painting and illustrations by Willem G. Van de Hulst, Jr.
Original translation done by Harry der Nederlanden for Paideia Press,
St. Catharines-Ontario-Canada.
The publisher expresses his appreciation to John Hultink of Paideia Press for
his generous permission to use his translation (ISBN 0-88815-511-5).

Edited by Mrs. Theresa Janssen and Paulina Janssen

ISBN 978-1-928136-11-8

Published simultaneously in U.S.A. by Inheritance Publications
Box 366, Pella, Iowa 50219

Printed in Canada

Contents

1. Look Out!

Swish! Out of the bushes tumbled a little boy. He looked very fierce. His face had a deep frown on it. He was walking very carefully, very slowly — step by step. He first peered one way and then the other. Look out! In his hand he was holding something very dangerous.

Swish! Another boy tumbled out of the bushes. He also looked very fierce. There was also a deep frown on his face. He looked around with beady eyes.

Look out! Under his arm he was carrying something dangerous.

Swish! Out of the bushes tumbled another boy. He was a fat little boy and he was trying to look fierce too. But he couldn't. He kept grinning. That was all wrong, so he bit his lip and puffed out his cheeks, trying to look fierce. He first peered one way and then the other. Look out! Across his shoulder he was carrying something dangerous. And on his head he was wearing an old army cap.

Shhh! . . . Shhh! . . . Step by step!
Quietly, very quietly, they tiptoed ahead, step by step. All three walked very carefully, very slowly. They bent their knees deep with every step. Slowly they crept through the woods. Look out! They looked very fierce and all of them were armed.
They were three brave little hunters. And when they shoot . . . !

2. Shoot Him!

Danny was out in front. He was the leader of the hunting party. He carried a pistol in his hand and had a box of bullets in his pocket. He had a big feather in his hair. That was to make him look fierce.

Behind him came Roger. Under his arm he carried a stick with a cross-piece nailed to it. That was his sword. He had wrapped a big rope around his waist — three times. That was to make him look fierce.

Last of all came fat Willy. He was wearing wooden shoes and carried a bow across his shoulder. Out of his pocket stuck an arrow. He set his army cap at an angle. That made him look even fiercer.

Danny whispered, "Come on. Let's hunt tigers, and bears, and elephants."
"I'll shoot them with my bow," said Willy.
Carefully they crept down the lane step by step. They were brave, fierce hunters.
They looked and they listened. Oh, if a bear came out of the woods — or a lion would spring out of the trees . . . they were ready. Let them come.

Suddenly, over there, under the hedge, something was rustling the leaves; something was parting the grass.

Suddenly, a kitten sprang from out of the bushes, a little gray kitten, a cute, playful kitten with a red ribbon around its neck. It saw the three boys and stopped in the middle of the lane.

The kitten was not afraid. Not at all. It thought the boys had come to play. It wriggled in excitement. The kitten was so excited, it held its little tail high in the air.

Poor little kitten! It did not know that the boys were fierce hunters. It did not know that they were armed and dangerous.

Bang! went Danny's cap gun. Bang!

The kitten shuddered with fright and squeezed its eyes.

"Shoot him! Shoot him!" shouted Danny. Bang! Bang! The bullets fell out of his pocket, but he did not see them. Bang! Bang! "Shoot him! Shoot him!"

Roger ran up, waving his sword. Willy tried to shoot too, but he got all tangled up in his bow and couldn't

8

find his arrow. So he used his cap instead. Whoosh!
He hurled his cap at the kitten. Plop! It landed right
on top of it.

Poor kitten! It tumbled head over heels. The little
thing was so frightened. Away it ran, back under the
hedge.
"Catch him! Catch him!" shouted Danny. Bang! Bang!
Roger whacked the branches with his sword. And
Willy dove at it. Missed! He just missed!

The kitten flew under the hedge. It hissed in fright.
Its little tail bristled in anger and it arched its back
like a bow.
Bang! Bang!
"Shoot him! Shoot him!" yelled Danny.

3. Behind the Hedge

Willy wriggled to crawl under the hedge. Foolish Willy! Look, on the other side he saw a big yard. In the yard stood a house with wide steps. A window was standing open. The sun shone into a pretty room. By the window stood a bed. And in the bed lay a little girl. Her cheeks were pale and her hands were so thin. She was sick — for a long time already.

She heard the boys shout. Startled, she sat up in bed and looked out the window. Oh, then she saw her dear little kitten run toward the house, its tail bristled in fright. Tears sprang into her eyes. "Here, Mabel!" she cried fearfully. "Here, Mabel! Run!"

Then she saw Willy's head come out from under the hedge. Angrily she shook her fist at him. "Go away!" she cried. "Leave my kitty alone. You bully!"

Willy laughed at her. Roger stuck his sword through the hedge. Danny pushed his head through the branches, aimed his pistol at her, and, bang! bang!

Oh, no! There came Alice, the housekeeper. She carried a broom. She was going to sweep the back steps. Oh, no! Alice saw the boys. Alice heard the girl's shouts. She became very angry.
"Get away from here, you bullies! Picking on a little kitten, are you? I'll teach you!"
She ran to the gate, still carrying her broom. Oh, no!

Danny ran away down the lane. So did Roger. But poor, fat little Willy! His head was stuck in the hedge. He tugged and tugged. His face turned bright red. Alice pulled the gate open. She was already in the lane.

Willy tugged hard. His head jerked free. "Ouch!" But Alice was already there, carrying her big broom. "Get away, you little bully! Picking on a little kitten, are you? And teasing sick little girls! Shame on you!" Willy scrambled to his feet. He shook with fear. "W-w-we were only playing hunters."

"Hunters, eh? Well, I'm a hunter too. Take that!" And she whacked the seat of his pants with her broom. It almost knocked him over. "Get, you little bully!" She threw his army cap after him.

Willy ran away as fast as his fat little legs could carry

him. He had blood on his cheeks. He had blood on his nose. That was because of the branches of the hedge.

4. Sally Ann

Mabel, the gray little kitten, was playing on Sally Ann's bed. The kitten was chasing its own tail. It was becoming very angry because its tail kept slipping away. It growled in anger.

The kitten had forgotten all about the three fierce little hunters. But not Sally Ann. She had not forgotten. Look! There were tears in her eyes.

Why? The three boys had been gone for a long time already. And her cute little kitten was playing on the bed. Why should she be sad?

Maybe because she could not go out and play? No, that was not it. Sally Ann was very patient and content.

Maybe because she felt sick? No, that was not it, either. Sally Ann was a very brave girl.

But why was Sally Ann so sad then?

Alice knew why. She felt sorry for Sally Ann. Alice said, "Listen, Sally Ann, I'll look once more: in the basement, in the attic, in the yard, even outside. I'll look everywhere."

Mother came into the room and sat down on Sally Ann's bed. She said, "Don't be sad, Sally Ann. I'll go look in the woods."

"Oh, Mother, what if those nasty boys find him! They

might hurt him. Maybe even kill him!"
Sally Ann wiped a big tear from her eyes. Mabel, the little kitten, pushed its soft little head against

Sally Ann's face. It wanted to play, but Sally Ann didn't feel like playing.

Alice knew why. She felt sorry for Sally Ann. Alice looked in the basement, in the attic, in the yard. She looked everywhere. She came back and said, "I can't find him anywhere."
Mother went to look in the woods. But she also came back and said, "I don't see him anywhere."
Mabel was sleeping in a little hollow on the bed. Sally Ann wiped another tear from her eyes.
Mother hugged Sally Ann and said, "Hush, Sally Ann, why is my little girl crying? All this time when you have been sick, you never cried. You don't know when you will be better, but our loving Father in heaven knows. You know the Lord is taking care of you. And He will make you better in His time. You always wait so patiently, that is good. The Lord never forgets you.

"Now you must not cry about your other kitten either. He has just wandered away and might come back any time. You must wait very patiently. That is good. Will you do that?"

"Yes, Mother. But . . . those nasty boys!"

5. Brave Hunters

The three little hunters were playing again. They had forgotten all about the cute little kitten. They had forgotten all about the sick little girl. All they thought about was the fun they were having.

They crept from tree to tree. If a lion or tiger would spring from the trees, they were ready.

Roger trailed behind. He searched the bushes carefully. Suddenly he stopped. His eyes lit up. He saw something on the ground among the dead leaves: an old shoe. "A bear! A bear!" He swung his sword. Whack! The bear was dead.

Danny ran up. Bang! Bang! He shot the bear with his pistol. But he was too late. The bear was already dead.

Willy put his arrow in his bow and fired. But his aim was off. The arrow flew high in the air. But bears do not fly.

No, the bear belonged to Roger. He was the one who had killed it.

Forward they went through the woods. Roger was out in front. Proudly he dragged the dead bear behind him on a piece of rope.

Along the path lay an old pan. Willy was the first to see it. He ran to it and shouted, "I know! Let's have cooked bear meat. Let's cook the bear in the pan. That will be fun!"

It was a very old pan. The bottom was rusted out. But that did not matter.

"Yes! Good idea," said Roger.

"Yes!" said Danny. "But what about me? I have to catch something too. Roger killed the bear and you found the pan. I haven't caught anything yet. You will have to help me."

They went on until they came to a small road. On the one side were the woods and on the other side a wide pasture. There were three cows in the pasture. But they could not get on the road because there was a small canal next to the pasture. There was a gate, but it was closed.

Bravely the three little hunters marched down the small road. Willy carried the pan under his arm and

16

Roger carried the bear on his back.

Danny said, "Let's make lots of noise. Like this: ksssst, ksssst! That will scare the animals out of the woods so we can shoot them. Maybe a real animal will come out. Maybe a rabbit — a real one!"

"Yes," said Roger, "a real one!"

"Right!" said Willy. "A big, live one!"

Their eyes shone.

"Let's go," said Danny. "Make lots of noise. Ksssst! Ksssst!"

Roger charged forward waving his sword. "Ksssst! Ksssst!"

Willy hit the bushes with his army cap, "Whoop! Whoop! Come on out, if you dare! Show yourselves! You don't dare! I will shoot you."

Suddenly . . . oh, what a fright. The bushes shook and the branches crackled. A large, ugly head pushed itself through the leaves. And then a foreleg appeared. The three boys froze in fright, such brave hunters they were. Willy dropped his cap in the grass. The pan under his arm shook.

And in the large, ugly head glistened two small beady eyes. They stared at the boys and glistened so brightly. Then another foreleg came out of the bushes. Oh, terrible. Those poor hunters.

The next moment the brave little hunters were running as fast as their legs could carry them.
Their knees shook with fear.
They ran and they ran. But the ugly beast was right behind them.

6. What a Strange Pan!

"Oink, oink! Wait! Why are you running away? Oink, oink! I'm hungry. I'm always hungry. Is there something good in that pan for me? Oink, oink! What is in that pan? Let me see! Let me taste it!

"Oink, oink! I escaped from my pen but the farmer did not see it. My trough was empty and I was hungry. I'm always hungry. Oink, oink! Wait. Won't you wait for me? Then I'll have to catch you — I want that pan with something good in it. I can run fast too. I want to see what's in that pan! Oink, oink, oink!"

Oh, it was a pig, a
huge, fat pig. It was
brown and had a
crooked black spot
around one eye. One of
its forelegs was also
black. It was a horribly
large pig and it could
run very fast. The

ground shook under its feet.
"Oink, oink!"
Oh, those poor, scared hunters.

They ran as fast as their legs could carry
them. They screamed in terror. Danny,
their leader, ran the fastest. Roger waved
his arms in fright and his sword too. The
dead bear bounced along on his back.
But where was fat little Willy?

Poor boy! He was too fat to run very fast. And it
was hard running fast on wooden shoes. The huge,
ugly pig was right behind him. It was after him
because he had the pan. Willy felt the ground shake,
the pig was so close.
"Help! Help!" he screamed.

He ran and ran. His round face was bright red with fright. Suddenly the pan slipped from his grasp. He tried to jump over it, but he missed, poor boy, and one of his feet landed right in the pan.

He tried to pull his foot out, but it was stuck. He tried to run with the pan on his foot, but that did not work either. Oh, no! Fat little Willy tripped and fell on his stomach. And the horrible pig was almost on top of him.

"Help! Help!" Oh, if the pig would bite . . . Quickly he rolled over, swinging his arms and legs wildly. The old pan still stuck to his foot.

The ugly pig pushed his brown snout forward, "Oink, oink! Hold still, will you? Let me see what's in the pan. Let me taste it.

"Oink, oink! Hold still! I'm hungry. The pans at the farm are all empty. Hold still! I'm hungry.

"Oink, oink! Ouch! Why did you do that? Why do you act so strange. Ouch!

Why did you hit me on the head with that pan?
Ouch!"
Willy thrashed and kicked wildly. Suddenly the pan
flew off his foot. But so did his wooden shoe. The
pan bounced away in the grass and the horrible pig
went after it. What a relief.

Willy scrambled to his feet. He ran away as fast as
he could — without his cap, without his pan, and
without one of his wooden shoes. But he did not
care, oh, no. As long as he was away, far away, from
that horrible beast. Away, away, far away.

The pig pushed its big snout into the pan, "Oink, oink! What's this? What a strange pan! You can look right through it. It's empty. What a shame! And I'm so hungry!

"Oink, oink! I'm going back home. They have better pans there. Maybe there will be some food in my trough. Oink!"

7. On the Gate

The three little hunters were sitting on the pasture gate. Willy was wearing his army cap again. His wooden shoe was back on his foot. And the pan was lying in the grass by the gate.

The pig was gone. All gone. They did not see it anywhere anymore. Carefully the boys had gone back and picked everything up: the pan, the wooden shoe, and the cap. Their fear was already beginning to fade. Danny was the leader of the hunting party. So he had to be brave. He said, "I'm not scared. If that pig comes back again, I'll shoot him with my pistol. Bang! Bang! He will roll over in fright."

"Right!" said Roger. "And I'll stab him with my sword. No, I have a better idea. I'll tie him up with my rope."

"No," said Willy. "I know. I'll put that pan on his head. He's afraid of that." He looked down the small

road and shouted, "You ugly pig! Come out if you dare. You don't dare. You don't dare. Oh, what is that?"

"Moo-oo-oo!"
The three brave little hunters almost fell off the gate in fright.
"Moo-oo-oo!" It was only a cow in the pasture.
The boys looked at each other. They laughed at their own fright. Then Willy turned around and stood up on the gate. Angrily he shouted at the cow, "What do you want? Come here if you dare! You're scared! I'll shoot you right through the heart."
The cow did not even look up. It just went on eating grass, taking one slow step after another: step . . . step . . . step.

Willy put his arrow in his bow. Twang! The arrow whizzed through the air. It landed just behind the cow. "I almost shot his tail off!" shouted Willy.

But the cow did not even look up. It just went on eating grass: step . . . step . . . step.

"Let's go," said Danny. "It's too dangerous here on the gate."

"Yes," said Roger. "Let's go."

"But what about my arrow?" asked Willy. "My arrow is out in the field."

Yes, that was true. It was too bad.

"Go get it," said Danny.

"Do you dare?" asked Willy.

"Not me," said Danny.

"Me neither," said Roger.

The cow wandered on: step . . . step . . . step.

Willy eyed it fearfully. "Should I?" he whispered. "Do you think it's safe?"

"Yes, go ahead!" whispered Danny and Roger. "It isn't dangerous. We'll wait for you — here, behind the gate."

Willy was very brave. He took off his wooden shoes and his cap and asked Roger to hold his bow for him. Then he climbed over the gate and tiptoed into the pasture. He crept forward as carefully, as quietly as he could, step by step. His fat cheeks shook with fear. What if that cow looked around?

But the cow didn't look back. It went on eating grass. Step . . . step . . . step.

Danny and Roger peered through the gate. Quietly they called to Willy, "Go on, Willy! Go on! Don't be afraid."

Willy saw his arrow in the grass. Just a few more steps. The cow wouldn't look up anymore anyway. One more step.

But suddenly Willy stopped. Why? He was no longer looking at the arrow and he forgot all about the cow. His eyes fastened on something very different. Oh, he stared wide-eyed.

What did he see?

8. How Did It Happen?

Willy forgot about his arrow. He forgot about the cow. All he thought about was what he saw in the grass. Very carefully, he went a little closer. It was white. It was . . . He started in surprise.
Willy looked back at the other boys by the gate. He waved his hand. Come! Come and see!

Danny climbed on top of the gate. "What is it? What do you see?" he shouted.
Roger peered through the gate. "Do you see something? What is it?" he shouted.
Willy did not dare to shout back. He just waved his hand. Come! Come and see!

Danny asked Roger, "Do you dare?"
And Roger asked Danny, "Do you dare?"

Both of them looked at the cow. The cow had moved farther into the pasture. It did not look up. It just went on eating grass. Carefully they climbed over the gate. They tiptoed forward over the grass. Finally they were beside Willy — both of them.

Willy pointed to the white thing in the grass, "Over there! Do you see it?"

Yes, Danny and Roger saw it. Their eyes, too, widened in surprise. They did not say anything. They just stared.

In the pasture stood a large tree. It had a huge trunk and spreading branches. Under the tree in the tall grass lay some big rocks. But that was not all, oh, no. Something was lying beside one of the big rocks. It was white, pure white, with a little blue. And . . . it moved.

The boys stood still.

It was very quiet. The leaves on the tree did not stir at all. The boys were silent.
In the stillness the boys heard it. Oh, do you hear it? There it was again: a tiny meow — like a cry of pain.

It was a kitten, a little white kitten — a pure white kitten with a blue ribbon around its neck.
But, oh, look! There was blood on its beautiful little white head. The kitten was bleeding. Poor kitten! What could have happened?
It lay against a big rock. There was also blood on the rock. The kitten lay very limp.
"Mew! Me-e-ew!" it cried softly. It was in pain. The tip of its little red tongue hung out of its mouth.
Poor kitten, what could have happened to it? Had it climbed up into the big tree? Had it crawled out onto a thin branch? And had it fallen out of the tree and banged its little head onto the big rock?

Oh, look! It moved one of its paws. But the other paw lay limp. The kitten could not even move it.
It quivered with pain.
The kitten tried to get up, but it could not.
Its soft, white body quivered.
"Mew! Me-e-ew!"

9. In Willy's Cap

Whose kitten could it be? Where did it come from? Was it dying? The three little hunters did not know. Now they had finally caught a real animal — a real, living animal. But they no longer thought of pistols and swords and arrows. They no longer thought of being brave and fierce. All they thought of was the poor kitten.

They felt very sorry for it, but they were also a little afraid of it. They shrank back from the sad eyes, the blood, and the pain.

Willy was the most daring. He stepped forward and gently prodded the kitten with his stocking foot. "Kitty. Here, Kitty. Come on!"

The kitten pulled up its little paws and opened its mouth, "Me-e-ew."

"Careful! Don't hurt him!" said Danny.

"I've got an idea!" said Roger, blushing with eagerness. "Let's take him along. Yes, oh, yes, let's take the kitty along."

Take it along? They looked at each other. Take it along? Yes, yes! They would take it along. What if that big cow came back and stepped on the little kitten!

"Yes, let's take him along, otherwise he will die. But how are we going to carry him?"

Willy had the answer, "In my pan!"

"In your pan? Your pan doesn't have a bottom. He will fall right through!"

"Oh, yes, I forgot."

"In my handkerchief!" said Roger.

But Danny had a better idea. "No, I know. In Willy's cap."

"In my cap?" said Willy. "Yes, yes! In my cap! That's good. Let's get it!"

The three little hunters dashed back to the gate to get the cap. They almost fell over each other in their haste. Then they ran back. They knelt down in the grass by the kitten. They laid the cap beside it.

"Careful!"

"Do you dare pick him up?"

"Let's do it all together," said Willy. "We'll lift him with our hands."

They put their hands side by side — all six of them.

30

They carefully, very carefully, slid them under the kitten.

It worked! Carefully they lifted the kitten off the ground. One of its legs dangled limply and the kitten mewed in pain. Together they lowered it into the cap. Then they picked handfuls of grass and put it into the cap with the kitten. That made a soft bed. Roger covered the kitten with his handkerchief. That was to keep it warm.

"Mew! Me-e-ew!" cried the kitten.

Willy was allowed to carry the kitten — it was his cap. That was fair.

"Oh, listen . . ." said Roger.

"Shhh! Quiet!" grumbled Willy. "Maybe the kitty will go to sleep. He needs to get better."

"Yes," said Danny. "Shhh!"

Danny led the way. He was the leader.

10. Is It True?

There they went, down the road back to town. There they went: three fierce little hunters and one hurt little kitten.

Willy, carrying the cap, walked in the middle. Roger carried Willy's bow. The arrow was still lying in the pasture and the pan was still lying by the gate. The dead bear still dangled from the rope on Roger's back. But the three boys had forgotten about the arrow and the pan and the bear. All they thought about was the kitten. They hurried along. Home was far away and they wanted to show the kitten to their parents. Willy was going to keep the kitten. That was fair. He had found it and it was lying in his cap.

But it was also Danny and Roger's kitten. They could come and play with it when it was better. That was also fair.

"Woof-woof!" Suddenly a dog came through a gate, barking and growling. Angrily it showed its teeth. Did the dog want their little kitten? Did it want to bite the kitten? Well, the little hunters were not scared off so easily. They would protect their kitten. They were frightened, but they stood their ground.

"Get away!" scolded Willy. He aimed a kick at the dog with his wooden shoe.

Roger waved the bow in one hand and the sword in the other. If that nasty dog tried to bite the kitten, he would . . . Danny put two caps in his pistol and held it right in front of the dog's nose. Bang!

That worked. The bang scared the dog terribly. It ran away with its tail between its legs. Oh, good.

On walked the three little hunters. Danny walked with his chest out. He had saved the kitten. He was a hero.

Oh, no!

There came dirty Harry. That could be dangerous! Dirty Harry worked for the blacksmith. He had a dirty face and dirty hands. And he was very strong. All the children were afraid of him. Oh, no! He eyed the three boys and the cap.

"What do you have in there? What's in that cap?"

"Nothing!"

"Let me see!"

"No!"

"No? Do you want me to throw all three of you in the canal? Give me that cap!"

His dirty hands reached for the cap. He yanked away the handkerchief. "Ha! A cat! Let me see."

"No! No! Keep your dirty hands off, you bully!" Danny grabbed him by the arm and Roger pulled on his jacket. Willy hid the cap against his body. "No! I won't give him to you. He's ours! You may not hurt him!"

"Me-e-ew! Me-e-ew!" went the kitten.

Dirty Harry laughed. "That

cat is already hurt. He's going to die anyway." Then he walked on, laughing. Oh, good.

But the three boys were frightened by his words. Was the kitten really going to die? Fearfully they stared at the hurt kitten. Gently they stroked it. The kitten stared back at them with its sad eyes. Its little red tongue quivered.

"Come on," said Willy. "My mother will put a bandage on his head. That will help. Come on!"

11. A Splint

A big car was parked beside the road. The three little hunters walked past it. The car was empty. But on the hood sat a little silver bird with long wings and tiny eyes made of red glass. The boys had seen the silver bird before: it belonged to the doctor's car.

"I have an idea!" said Roger. He blushed with eagerness and his eyes shone. "Listen, listen!" The boys stopped and put their heads close together. Roger whispered.

"Yes, yes! That's what we will do! Oh, yes!"

"Yes, but you will have to ask, Roger."

"All right," said Roger.

They looked up and down the street, but saw no one. So they sat down on the bumper of the car to wait.

Willy sat in the middle with the cap in his lap. The kitten lay very, very still. Was it sleeping? Or was it dead? It lay so quietly. Lifting up one corner of the handkerchief, they fearfully peered into the cap. The kitten's eyes were closed.

They waited a long time. But suddenly Danny cried, "Oh, look, there he comes! Come on!" He poked Willy and Willy quickly stood up.

Roger blushed with fear. Sure enough, down the driveway came the doctor. The doctor looked angry. He thought, "What are those boys doing by my car? Were they playing on it? Did they make it dirty?" And now, look, they dare come toward him, the bold little

rascals! He eyed them angrily through his glasses. But they walked right up to the doctor, Roger in front. He blushed with fear.

Danny poked him, "Go ahead, ask him!"

But Roger was afraid. The doctor looked so angry. Still, he had said he would. Suddenly he put up his hand and said, "D-D-Doctor, will you . . . will you please make our kitty better?"

The doctor's eyes widened in surprise. "What? What's that you say? What do you want me to do?"

"Please, Doctor, Dirty Harry says our kitty is dying. He got hurt when he fell. Would you please make him better, Doctor?"

"But I'm not a vet. I don't treat animals." The anger left the doctor's eyes and he even smiled a little. He looked in the cap. He lifted the kitten's head a little. He felt the limp leg.

"Hmm!" he said. "Hmm! That head doesn't look too bad. But that leg . . . that leg is broken. We have to put a splint on it."

The doctor took out a knife. The boys shrank back in fright. The cap shook in Willy's hands. But the knife was not meant for the kitten. The doctor used it to cut a piece of wood off Roger's sword. Why? Ah, then . . .

Then the doctor sat down on the bumper of his car. "Come here with that kitten." He took the kitten on his knee and said, "Hold him. Hold him very still. Otherwise he will scratch me."

Oh, look, the doctor took the stick he had cut from Roger's sword and held it along the kitten's broken leg.

Then he tied Roger's handkerchief around the stick and the leg. The kitten squealed in pain. It tried to bite and it tried to scratch, but the boys held it still. Their hands shook.

"Good!" said the doctor. "Good! It's done. Now the leg will heal. You can put the kitten back in the cap. Good! Take good care of him."

"Yes, yes, we will, Doctor."

"Would you boys like a ride? Come on then. Climb in. We'll bring our patient home fast."

He pushed the three little hunters into his car.

Toot-toot! Vrrroom! Away they went. Toot-toot! The boys fell against each other as the doctor turned a corner. Vrrroom! But the boys held on tightly to the cap — all three of them. They had to take good care of the kitten.

12. Angry Alice

The car stopped in front of a beautiful house. The doctor went inside. He asked the boys to wait. Was someone sick in the beautiful house?

Danny said, "Didn't we go fast?"

"We sure did! " said Roger.

"We sure did!" said Willy. "I think the kitten liked the ride too, it bounced around in my cap."

The doctor walked to a big room in the back of the house. In front of the open window stood a bed. And in the bed lay a little girl. Her cheeks were so pale and her hands were so thin. On the covers slept a little kitten — a gray kitten with a red ribbon around its neck.

The girl looked up sadly.

The doctor said, "What's this? Why so sad? Don't you hear the birds singing in the back yard? You are getting stronger every day. Soon you will be in the back yard with the birds. My, you have a pretty

kitten. When did you get her? Who gave her to you?"
The doctor petted the kitten. The kitten woke up and
rolled over on its back. It grabbed the doctor's big
hand with its four small paws. Playfully it bit at his
fingers. The doctor laughed.
But the sick little girl . . . she got tears in her eyes.
Again the doctor asked, "What's the matter? Why
are you so sad?"
The girl's mother said, "Doctor, shall I tell you why
Sally Ann is so sad?"

Alice, the housekeeper, walked by in the hall. She
was going outside to polish the doorknob and the
doorbell. Under her arm was a basket with rags. She
opened the front door wide.
What was this? Look!?! Three strange boys were
sitting in the doctor's beautiful car! The bold rascals!

40

Why, they were the same boys she had chased away
— the ones that had been picking on the kitten!
Then she saw the cap. And in the cap . . . ! Oh,
suddenly Alice became angry. She became very angry.
She ran to the car. She poked Danny in the shoulder,
she tugged Roger's hair, and she whacked Willy with
one of her rags.

"You nasty boys! You bullies! Look, that poor kitten!
Oh, no! There's blood on his head. And what's that
big bulge on his leg?

"You did that, you mean little bullies! Oh, I should . . .
I should . . . !

"And Sally Ann was so sad that her other kitten got
lost. He wandered away from home yesterday and
couldn't find his way back. The poor little thing!

"But you nasty boys got your hands on it. Look at
him. What did you do to him? You almost killed him!

41

Give me that kitten! Oh, I should . . . I should . . . !"
She snatched the cap out of Willy's hands and put
the kitten in her apron.

"Get, you bullies. Out of that car!" She yanked the
boys out of the car. Willy's cap and Roger's sword
went flying. Her polishing rags blew across the street.
Then she rushed back to the house with the kitten
wrapped in her apron.

Just then, the doctor was leaving. But Alice did not
see him. She was so angry. She ran right into him.
"Oh, Doctor! Excuse me, I . . . I . . ."

13. Like a Party

Poor boys! Poor little hunters! They really had not
deserved that. But, the doctor had seen everything.
He stopped Alice. Angrily he said to her, "Foolish
woman, what are you doing? You shook up those
boys. You threw away their toys. You chased them
out of the car. You scolded them. And what for?"

"They're bullies. Look what they did to this poor
kitten."

"Bullies? They're nothing of the kind. They didn't
hurt that kitten. Quite the opposite. They are brave
little men. They saved that kitten. I'm proud of
them!"

Alice's eyes widened in surprise.

"That's right!" said the doctor. "Don't pull such a funny face. They are good boys. I'll fix it all up. Come on in, boys — all three of you. Take your cap and sword and bow along. Come on in. Yes, it's all right. Did Alice scare you? Ha-ha-ha! Don't worry, I'll protect you from her. I'll fix it all up."

Look, the doctor sat down beside Sally Ann's bed again. So did Mother. All three of them were laughing. The doctor had told Sally Ann the whole story. He said, "Sally Ann, your pretty white kitten is no longer lost. I know where he is. But he was hurt a little. One of his legs is bandaged. He fell out of a tall tree. But it isn't serious. Soon he will be better again. Three brave little boys saved him. And Alice scolded them and whacked them with her polishing rag for their troubles. Ha-ha-ha!"

Sally Ann kept looking at the door. What was keeping the kitten? Ah, the door was opening . . .

In marched the brave little hunters — all three of them. First Willy — on his stocking feet. He had a black smudge on his nose. That was from Alice's polishing rag. He was carrying the cap with the kitten in it. The kitten's white little head peeked over the edge. The blood had been washed off.
Then followed Danny with the bow and Roger with

half a sword. And the dead bear still dangled
from the rope on Roger's back.

Behind them came Alice. She looked a little
flustered but she was smiling anyway.

Oh, Sally Ann was so happy, she bounced up and
down in bed. It was just like a parade!

Willy put the kitten down on Sally Ann's bed. Sally
Ann put a new blue ribbon around its neck. The kitten
looked much happier already. Its leg was very stiff,
but it didn't hurt anymore.

The three little hunters sat around the bed — each
on a stool — in a circle. Alice brought them each a

44

tall glass of pink lemonade and a big piece of cake. That was to make up for frightening them. Then the boys had to tell the others the whole story: about the pig and the pan and the dog and dirty Harry.

It was just like a party.

14. Thankfulness

There went the three little hunters again. The doctor gave them a ride to the church. Then they were on their way home. Willy still had the black smudge on his nose and Roger still carried the dead bear on his back.

All they thought of was the fun they were going to have. Oh, yes, the next day they were allowed to play in Sally Ann's big back yard. Sally Ann could not play with them. Not yet. But soon she would be better. And they were going to get lemonade and cake again. Sally Ann's mother had said so.

"I'm going to take my pistol along," said Danny.
"And I'm taking my bow."
"And I'm going to make a new sword."
"But we're not going to hunt kittens."
"No, of course not!"
"Never!"

The kittens — Mabel and Sam — were sleeping side by side in their basket. Sam's head was resting on his bandaged leg.

Sally Ann lay with her head on Mother's shoulder. She smiled and her eyes sparkled. "Oh, Mother, I'm so happy!" she said.

Mother smiled too. She said, "Didn't I tell you? We must always be patient, the Lord never forgets us. He knows everything."

"Yes, Mother," Sally Ann whispered softly.

"You were afraid those nasty boys would find your kitten. You thought they might kill him. But it was just the opposite. They were good, brave boys. They saved Sam. See, Sally Ann? We must always be patient. The Lord in heaven knows everything."

"Yes, Mother," Sally Ann quietly answered. "Oh, Mother, and tomorrow the boys are coming again. I can watch them play through my open window. Then

it's almost like I'm playing with them, isn't it, Mother? And pretty soon, when I get a little stronger and then a little stronger again . . . Oh, Mother, then I can go out and play with them. Will you ask them to come again?"

"Of course, Sally Ann."

Then it became very quiet in the room. Mother did not say anything and Sally Ann did not say anything either. Sally Ann's bright blue eyes looked out into the back yard. She looked between the trees up to the blue sky beyond — the blue sky that was so high and so far. And Sally Ann whispered something, very, very softly. Mother could not even hear what she said.

She said, "Dear Lord, I'll be very patient." And her blue eyes sparkled with happiness.

Titles in this series: